Inside the NFL

THE
NEW ENGLAND PATRIOTS

BOB ITALIA
ABDO & Daughters

Published by Abdo & Daughters, 4940 Viking Drive, Suite 622, Edina, Minnesota 55435.

Copyright © 1996 by Abdo Consulting Group, Inc., Pentagon Tower, P.O. Box 36036, Minneapolis, Minnesota 55435 USA. International copyrights reserved in all countries. No part of this book may be reproduced in any form without written permission from the publisher.

Printed in the United States.

Cover Photo credits: Wide World Photos/Allsport Photos
Interior Photo credits: Wide World Photos, pages 4-9, 11, 14, 17-20, 23, 24, 26
Bettmann Photos, pages 12, 16, 18, 19
Allsport Photos, page 21

Edited by Kal Gronvall

Library of Congress Cataloging-in-Publication data

Italia, Bob, 1955
The New England Patriots / Bob Italia.
    p. cm. — (Inside the NFL)
    Includes index.
Summary: A brief history of the players, coaches, and games of one of the best teams in the National Football League.
    ISBN 1-56239-467-3
1. New England Patriots (Football team)—Juvenile literature. 2. National Football League—Juvenile literature. [1. New England Patriots (Football team)—History. 2. Football—History.] I. Title. II. Series Italia, Bob, 1955- Inside the NFL.
GV956.N36I83   1995
796.332'64'0974461--dc20   95-16471
                                                                           CIP
                                                                           AC

CONTENTS

Flirting with Greatness 4

The Boston Patriots 6

Plunkett 9

The Stingley Tragedy 13

The Berry Era 15

Slipping 17

Parcells and Bledsoe 21

The 1994 Season 22

Glossary 29

Index 31

Flirting with Greatness

The Patriots have flirted with greatness only once in their short history. Players such as Steve Grogan, Andre Tippett, Stanley Morgan, Irving Fryar, and Michael Haynes gave the Patriots a miraculous 1985 season which brought an AFC championship. Since that time, the Patriots have endured some of the worst times in club history.

All that is about to change, however. Coach Bill Parcells has brought his winning ways to New England, and has assembled a team that is poised on the brink of greatness.

Leading the way is a strong-armed quarterback named Drew Bledsoe. Having already established NFL passing records, Bledsoe is destined to bring a championship to New England for the first time in its history.

Coach Bill Parcells of the New England Patriots.

Drew Bledsoe leading the Patriots, 1995.

The Boston Patriots

The Boston Patriots formed in 1960 as one of the eight original members of the American Football League (AFL). Boston had some success early on. Quarterback Babe Parilli, wide receiver Gino Cappelletti, and linebacker Nick Buoniconti were among their star players.

In 1963, the Patriots tied the Buffalo Bills for first place in the division. In the playoffs, they defeated the Bills 26-8. Boston then played the San Diego Chargers for the AFL title. The Chargers destroyed the Patriots 51-10.

In 1964, the Patriots finished second, losing the division title to Buffalo in the season's final game. Looking to improve their rushing attack, the Patriots chose University of Syracuse running back Jim Nance in the college draft.

Nance entered the Patriots' 1965 training camp weighing 260 pounds—more than most linemen. But Nance was fast for his size. Coach Mike Holovak gave Nance a shot at running back instead of converting him to a lineman.

At first, Nance did not do well. Holovak gave him a choice. If he didn't get his weight down, he would work out with the linemen.

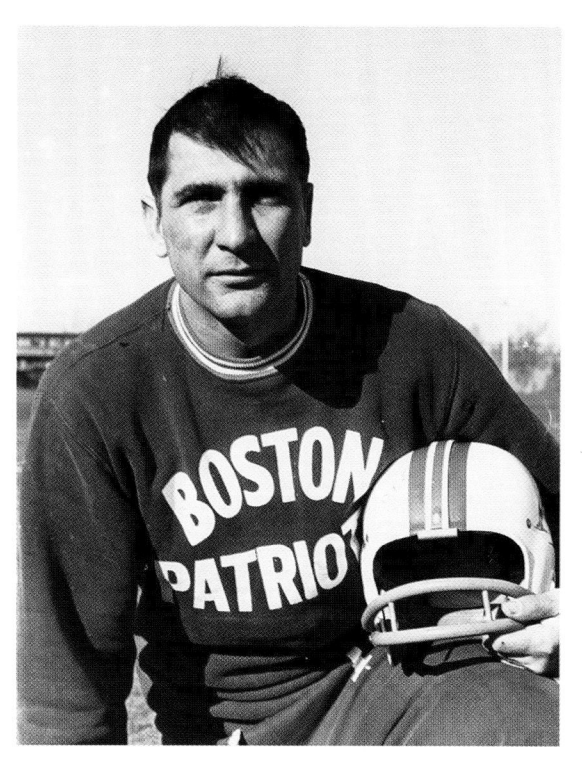

Babe Parilli, quarterback of the Boston Patriots in the early 1960s.

Nick Buoniconti of the Boston Patriots, 1963.

    Nance did not want to play guard. He lost 14 pounds in one week and soon regained his starting fullback position.

    In 1965, Boston slumped to 4-8-2. It was the team's worst record in its first six years. Thirty-four-year-old Babe Parilli threw 26 interceptions. Nance was still battling his weight problem, and was ineffective.

But when the 1966 training camp opened, Nance was a "slim" 235 pounds. That season, he gained an AFL-record 1,458 yards. The Patriots nearly won the division. Nance was now one of the most feared backs in the league.

But in 1967, the Patriots finished 3-10-1 and fell to last place. They would stay at the bottom of the division for many years to come.

When the AFL and NFL merged in 1970, the Patriots did not have a home stadium. There was no place in Boston for them to play. They were forced to play at Harvard University in Cambridge, Massachusetts. In 1971, however, the Patriots finally found a home—at Schaefer Stadium in nearby Foxboro, Massachusetts. As a result, owner Billy Sullivan changed the team name to the New England Patriots.

Jim Nance, 1966.

Plunkett

It would take many years—and good players—to return the Patriots to their winning ways. The Patriots took the first step when they signed quarterback Jim Plunkett in 1971.

In his first regular-season NFL game, Plunkett threw two touchdown passes as the Patriots won 20-6 over the Oakland Raiders. Plunkett played well the entire season and led New England to a 6-8-0 record.

The next season, however, the offensive line had many holes, and Plunkett took a pounding. Head coach John Mazur and general manager Upton Bell feuded all season about how to rebuild the team. As a result, New England finished 3-11-0. Afterwards, Mazur quit and Bell left the team. The Patriots were in turmoil.

To get the team back on track, New England signed Chuck Fairbanks as head coach in 1973. Then, to rebuild the offensive line, they signed John Hannah. He was six feet two inches tall and weighed 270 pounds. Hannah was strong, quick and athletic. He greatly improved the pass blocking, and gave Plunkett more time to throw the ball to rookie wide receiver Darryl Stingley.

Quarterback Jim Plunkett took over in 1971.

Another rookie, running back Sam Cunningham, bolstered the running game. With their improved team, the Patriots finished 5-9.

The Patriots continued to rebuild their team with quality players. In 1975, New England chose tight end Russ Francis in the first round of the college draft. Francis was six-feet, six-inches tall and weighed 242 pounds. Even more, he was an outstanding pass catcher.

Unfortunately for New England, Plunkett had trouble getting the ball to Francis—or any of his receiving corps. After a good first year, Plunkett was having difficulties completing passes. When New England finished 3-11 in 1975, the Patriots decided to trade Plunkett to the San Francisco 49ers. Now, Steve Grogan was the starting quarterback.

The Patriots had a spring camp in late May 1976. When Grogan came in, he was the only quarterback who had been with the Patriots the year before. Even more, he was the only one who knew the offensive system.

The quarterback change worked wonders. In 1976, Grogan led the Patriots to an 11-3 record and a wildcard berth in the playoffs. The dramatic turnaround helped earn Fairbanks Coach of the Year honors.

Besides Grogan, other players contributed to the Patriots' success. Cornerback Mike Haynes finished second in the AFC in punt return average and interceptions, and was named Defensive Rookie of the Year. Francis had another outstanding year and was considered the NFL's best tight end. As a team, the Patriots led the NFL in yards per rush and were second in scoring. They also had a league-best 50 takeaways.

In the first round of the playoffs, New England played the Raiders in Oakland. The Patriots jumped out to a 21-10 lead in the second half. But Oakland quarterback Kenny Stabler rallied the Raiders to a 24-21 win. It was a disappointing loss. But the young New England Patriots were a team on the rise.

In 1977, the Patriots added two more star players from the 1977 college draft. Raymond Clayborn was a running back from the

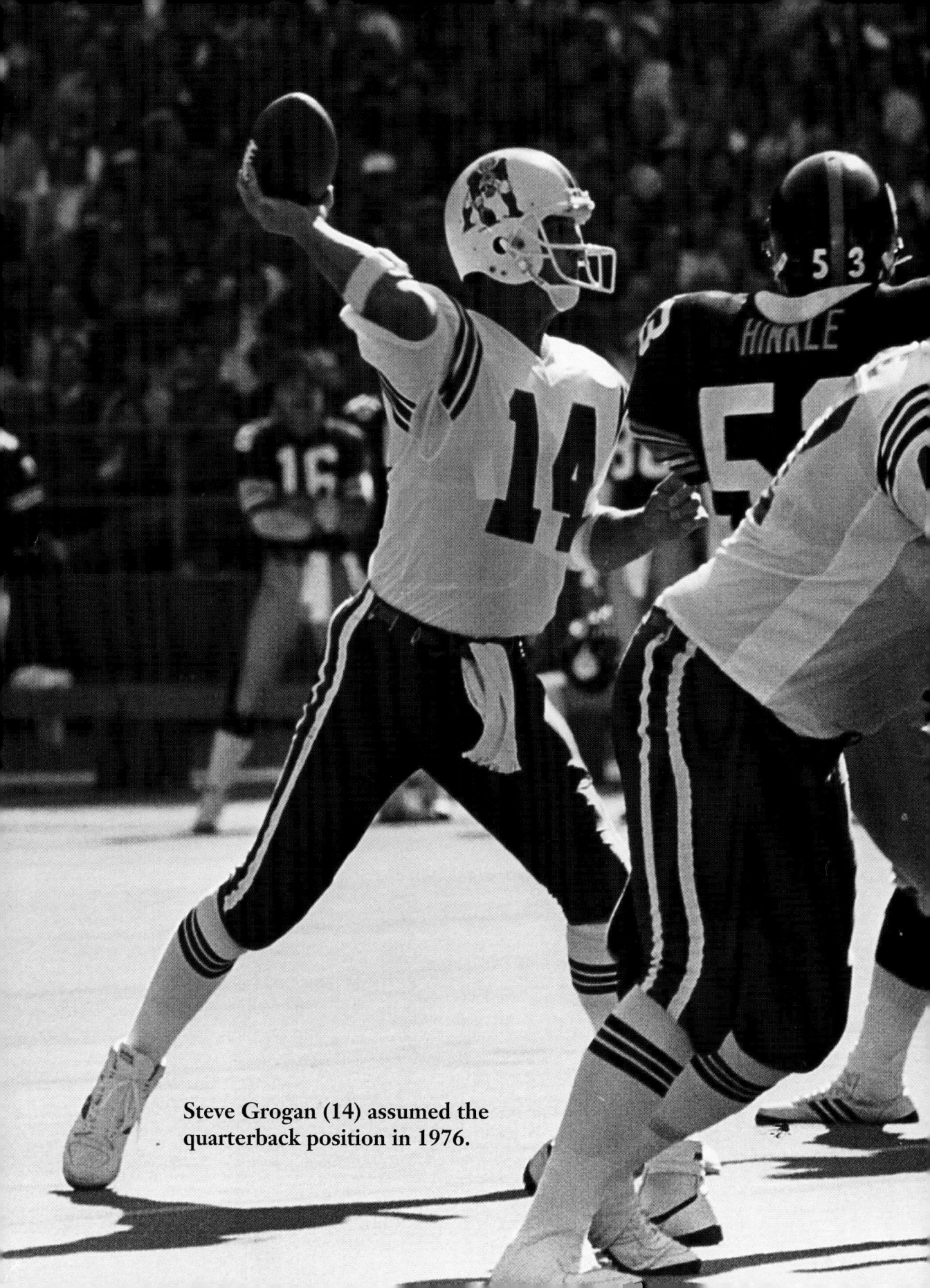

Steve Grogan (14) assumed the quarterback position in 1976.

University of Texas. The Patriots took him as a cornerback. He blended well with Haynes and soon became one of the best pass defenders in the league.

Wide receiver Stanley Morgan was a world-class sprinter while at the University of Tennessee. His impact on the team—and the rest of the NFL—was immediate.

With all their talent, the Patriots expected to make the Super Bowl in 1977. But Hannah and fellow lineman Leon Gray held out for more money. Hannah eventually returned to the Patriots' starting lineup. But Gray was traded to the New Orleans Saints. As a result, the players became bitter, and it affected their play.

The Super Bowl was no longer an issue. The Patriots lost four games early in that season and never recovered. A late-season rally allowed them to finish 9-5. But they did not make the playoffs.

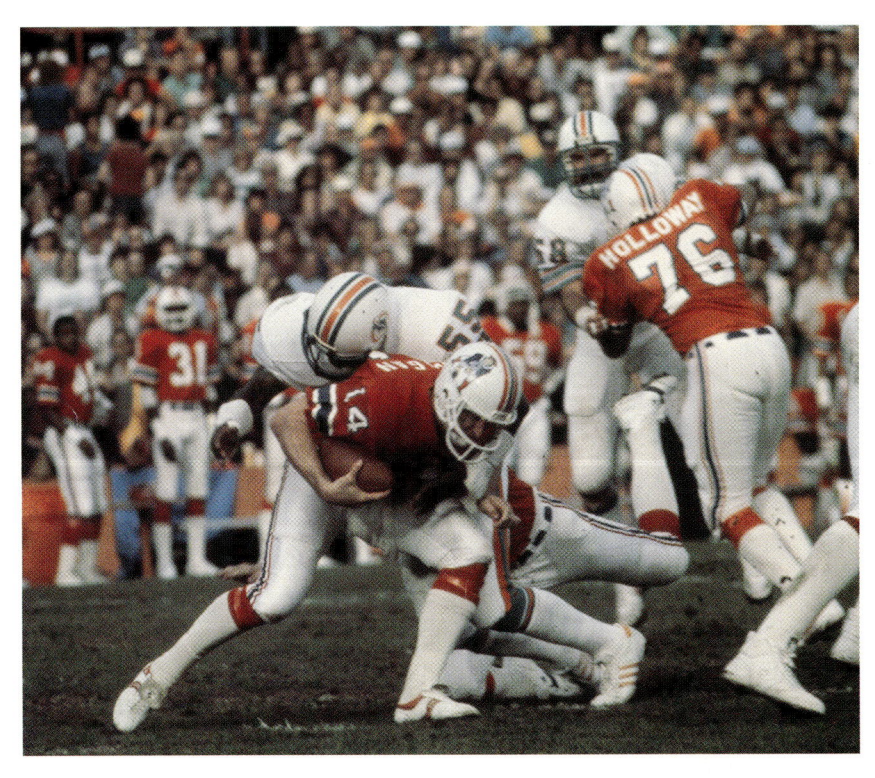

Quarterback Steve Grogan being sacked by a Miami defender.

The Stingley Tragedy

Talk of the Super Bowl returned in 1978 as New England was favored to win the AFC championship. But tragedy struck during a preseason game against the Raiders in Oakland.

Grogan threw a pass to Stingley over the middle. He jumped high into the air—and collided with defensive back Jack Tatum. Stingley crumpled to the ground and lay motionless on the field.

Doctors rushed onto the field. Stingley was carefully placed on a stretcher and taken to a nearby hospital. X-rays showed that Stingley's neck was broken. He was paralyzed from the shoulders down.

The Patriots dedicated the 1978 season to their fallen star receiver. New England won the AFC Eastern Division with a 11-5 record. But in the playoffs, the Houston Oilers defeated the Patriots 31-14 in Foxboro. Afterwards, Fairbanks left the team to coach the University of Colorado.

Ron Erhardt replaced Fairbanks. He lasted three years as the talent-rich Patriots failed to make the playoffs. In 1981, the Patriots hit rockbottom with a 2-14 record. It was time for a change.

Ron Meyer became head coach in 1982. Meyer immediately traded Francis, Rod Shoate, and Tim Fox for draft choices which Meyer would use to rebuild the defense. In the college draft, Meyer selected defensive lineman Kenneth Sims of the University of Texas and linebacker Andre Tippett of the University of Iowa.

The following season, Meyer made more changes. He drafted Tony Eason who battled Grogan for the starting quarterback job. Despite the new talent, New England could not make it to the playoffs. Sullivan fired Meyer during the 1984 season and promoted assistant coach Raymond Berry to the head coaching position.

Tony Eason battled Grogan for the starting quarterback position.

The Berry Era

Raymond Berry was a former All-Pro wide receiver with the Baltimore Colts. He had worked wonders with Stingley and Morgan. The Patriots hoped he could work wonders for the entire team.

In 1985, Tony Eason began the season at quarterback but was injured. Grogan replaced him—and began playing his best ball ever. With the strong running of Craig James and the pass catching of Morgan and Irving Fryar, the Patriots suddenly found themselves in the playoff hunt.

New England finished with an impressive 11-5 record. Though they did not win their division, the Patriots made the playoffs.

In postseason play, Berry used the running game against opponents. Eason replaced Grogan, but he rarely threw the ball. James and fellow running back Tony Collins were the stars in playoff victories over the New York Jets, Los Angeles Raiders, and Miami Dolphins. Incredibly, the wildcard Patriots had made it to the Super Bowl.

New England fans hoped the playoff magic would continue in the Super Bowl against the powerful Chicago Bears. The Patriots had an opportunistic defense that forced opponents into many mistakes and turnovers. The Patriots hoped the Bears—losers of only one game all season—would self-destruct in the big game.

But New England's luck had run out. After a first-quarter Walter Payton fumble, the Bears regrouped and played a solid, mistake-free game the rest of the way. The Bears went on to trounce the Patriots 46-10. New England's best season ever had ended in a total collapse. But they were still young and talented, and had a bright future ahead of them.

In 1986, however, the Patriots had one major question regarding 30-year-old Stanley Morgan. Morgan had struggled with injuries during the 1984 and 1985 seasons. No one knew if he would ever be healthy enough to play well again.

That season, Morgan answered his critics by setting Patriots' receiving records. He caught 84 passes—a team record—including 10 touchdown passes. Even more, he had 9 games with at least 100 yards receiving. It was his best year ever.

Morgan's biggest catch came in the final regular-season game—a game the Patriots needed to win to make the playoffs. With 44 seconds remaining, New England was tied with Miami. The Patriots had the ball on the Dolphin 30-yard line.

Under Raymond Berry, Steve Grogan played his best football ever.

Grogan dropped back and tossed the ball up the right sideline to Morgan. Morgan ran under it and caught the ball for a touchdown. The Patriots had a dramatic victory—and won a playoff berth.

The Patriots traveled to Denver's Mile High Stadium to face John Elway and the Broncos. New England took the lead in the fourth quarter. But Elway engineered a late touchdown drive that gave Denver a 22-17 victory. It was Raymond Berry's last playoff game with New England. And even worse, John Hannah decided to retire. The Patriots were at the crossroads. No one knew exactly what to expect in the following season.

Slipping

Much to their fans' dismay, the Patriots slipped in 1987 and 1988. But in 1989, playoff hopes had returned. The 1988 team had the NFL's fifth-best defense with many star players. Linebacker Andre Tippett was compared to New York Giants' linebacker Lawrence Taylor. He could rush the passer, haul down the swiftest running backs—even defend against speedy wide receivers.

Tippett wasn't the only defensive success story. Cornerback Ronnie Lippett developed into one of the NFL's best pass defenders. Defensive linemen Brent Williams and Garin Veris added to the fearsome pass rush. In 1988, Williams finished tenth in the AFC in sacks.

On offense, rookie running back John Stephens rushed for 1,168 yards—second in the AFC. He also was named to the Pro Bowl.

But in 1989, New England suffered more bad luck. Tippett, Lippett, and Veris were lost for the year in New England's final preseason game. On offense, Stevens was slowed by injuries. Morgan missed six games with a broken leg, and wide receiver Irving Fryar missed five games. New England's 5-11 record could not save Raymond Berry's job.

Defensive coordinator Rod Rust was promoted to head coach. But in 1990, the Patriots suffered through one of the worst seasons ever experienced by an NFL team. Fryar and Hart Lee Dykes were

Patriot linebacker Andre Tippett hauls down Seattle Seahawks quarterback Dave Krieg.

17

NEW ENGLAND PATRIOTS

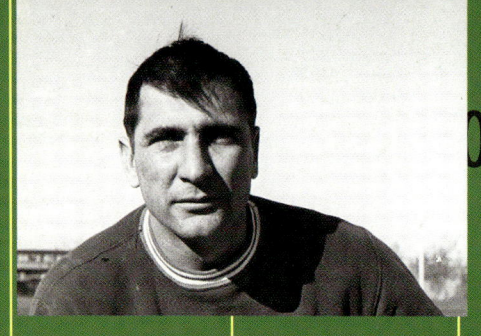

Babe Parilli is quarterback of the Boston Patriots in 1960.

Nick Buoniconti plays for the Boston Patriots in 1963.

Jim Plunkett signs with the Patriots in 1971.

Steve Grogan gets his first start at quarterback in 1976.

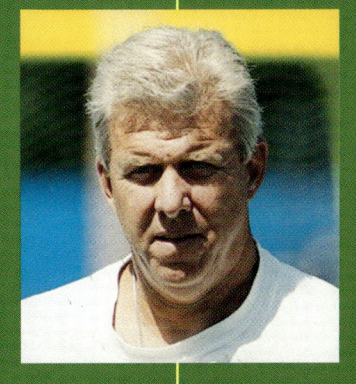

Bill Parcells becomes head coach in 1993.

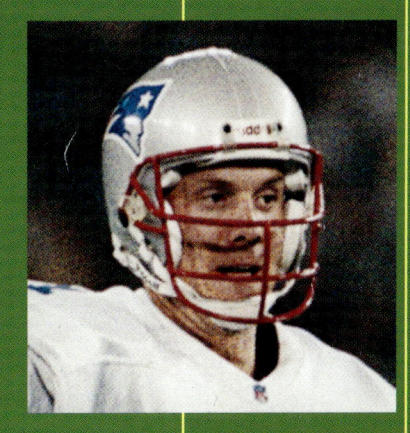

Drew Bledsoe is drafted in 1993.

Tony Eason leads his team to the Super Bowl in the 1985 season.

NEW ENGLAND PATRIOTS

injured. Grogan suffered a neck injury. The offense was nonexistent. The 1-15 Patriots scored only 181 points the entire year—the fewest points by any team since the 16-game schedule began. Rust was fired at the end of the season.

In 1991, new head coach Dick MacPherson came over from Syracuse University and fired up the Patriots. His approached worked, as New England finished 6-10. Hugh Millen was the new quarterback and passed for 3,073 yards. Fryar had his best season ever with 1,014 receiving yards. Tight end Marv Cook caught an NFL-best 82 receptions. Even more, Leonard Russell was the NFL Offensive Rookie of the Year as he rushed for 959 yards.

Too much was expected of the Patriots the following season. They failed to improve on last season's record. MacPherson was hospitalized with a serious illness and missed seven games. The Patriots started four different quarterbacks—none of whom performed well. New England had only 1,550 yards rushing and six rushing touchdowns as they finished 2-14.

Foxboro Stadium, home of the New England Patriots.

Parcells and Bledsoe

MacPherson was replaced by Bill Parcells. Parcells had won two Super Bowls with the New York Giants. Hope was restored, but Parcells had a lot of work to do.

Parcells' first move was to choose quarterback Drew Bledsoe in the 1993 draft. Bledsoe quickly became the starter. The Patriots lost their first four games. After winning one game, they lost seven more. Then things began to jell. New England closed out the season with four wins in a row. Bledsoe passed for 2,494 yards and 15 touchdowns. Leonard Russell rushed for 1,088 yards and 7 touchdowns. After the season, the team was sold to Robert Kraft, owner of Foxboro Stadium. In just one year, Parcells had the Patriots on the rise.

Drew Bledsoe, the Patriots quarterback of the future.

The 1994 Season

In the first game of the 1994 season at Miami, Bledsoe and the Dolphins Dan Marino hooked up in a passing duel. The Patriots led most of the game, and got 421 passing yards and 4 touchdowns from their strong-armed quarterback. Tight end Ben Coates had 16- and 63-yard scoring catches. But the Dolphins prevailed 39-35.

The next week, it was more of the same madness against the Buffalo Bills. Bledsoe passed for 380 yards and 3 touchdowns. But New England fell 38-35. After two weeks, the Patriots led the NFL in scoring and total offense. But they were 0-2. Still, Patriots fans were excited about the whirlwind start. So was the rest of the NFL.

"The Patriots are a heck of a team," Bills quarterback Jim Kelly said after the game. "Bledsoe is going to be great. Not good. Great."

The following week, Bledsoe's 34-yard touchdown pass to Michael Timpson pushed the Patriots to a 31-28 win over the Cincinnati Bengals. It was Bledsoe's club-record fourth straight 300-yard game. Bledsoe completed 30 of 50 passes for 365 yards. Timpson and Ben Coates each went over 100 yards receiving. The Patriots seemed to have finally turned the corner.

In Week 4, the Bledsoe magic continued. He passed for 251 yards as New England controlled the ball for nearly 35 minutes in a 23-17 victory over the Detroit Lions. Then, the following week, the Patriots won their third game in a row by edging the Green Bay Packers 17-16 in Foxboro. Matt Bahr's 33-yard, line-drive field goal, which barely cleared the crossbar, won the game with four seconds left.

"The only thing nice about it was that it went through," Bahr said.

Bledsoe passed for 334 yards—his fourth 300-yard game in five starts. He also led the game-winning drive. It began on the New

England 40 after Green Bay's kickoff sailed out of bounds for a penalty. His 10-yard pass to Ray Crittenden put the ball at the 15-yard line.

"I've always felt comfortable in the two-minute offense because you can get into a rhythm,' Bledsoe said. "There's an attitude on the team now that hasn't been there before. We expect to win."

Fourteen of the Patriots' last fifteen games had been decided by six or fewer points. They had won six of those last eight close games.

In Week 6, the Patriots dropped a 21-17 game to the Raiders. Then they lost 24-17 to the New York Jets. Receiving a bye in Week 8, the Patriots were 3-4 in the tough AFC East—but only two games behind Miami.

Head coach Bill Parcells.

Hopes were still running high in the rematch against Dan Marino and the first-place Dolphins. But this time, it wasn't even close. Bledsoe, who started the day as the NFL leader in passing yards, threw for just 125 yards and three interceptions as Miami won 23-3 in Foxboro. The fans began grumbling.

Week 10 brought no relief. Winds gusting to 40 miles per hour and rain hindered the top-ranked passing game of Bledsoe. He threw for 166 yards, nearly half of it in the fourth quarter, and was intercepted four times. The Patriots lost 13-6 to Cleveland, and found themselves in last place with a 3-6 mark—four games behind Miami.

In the Week 11 match against Minnesota, the Patriots fell behind 20-0 in the second quarter. With less than three minutes left in the

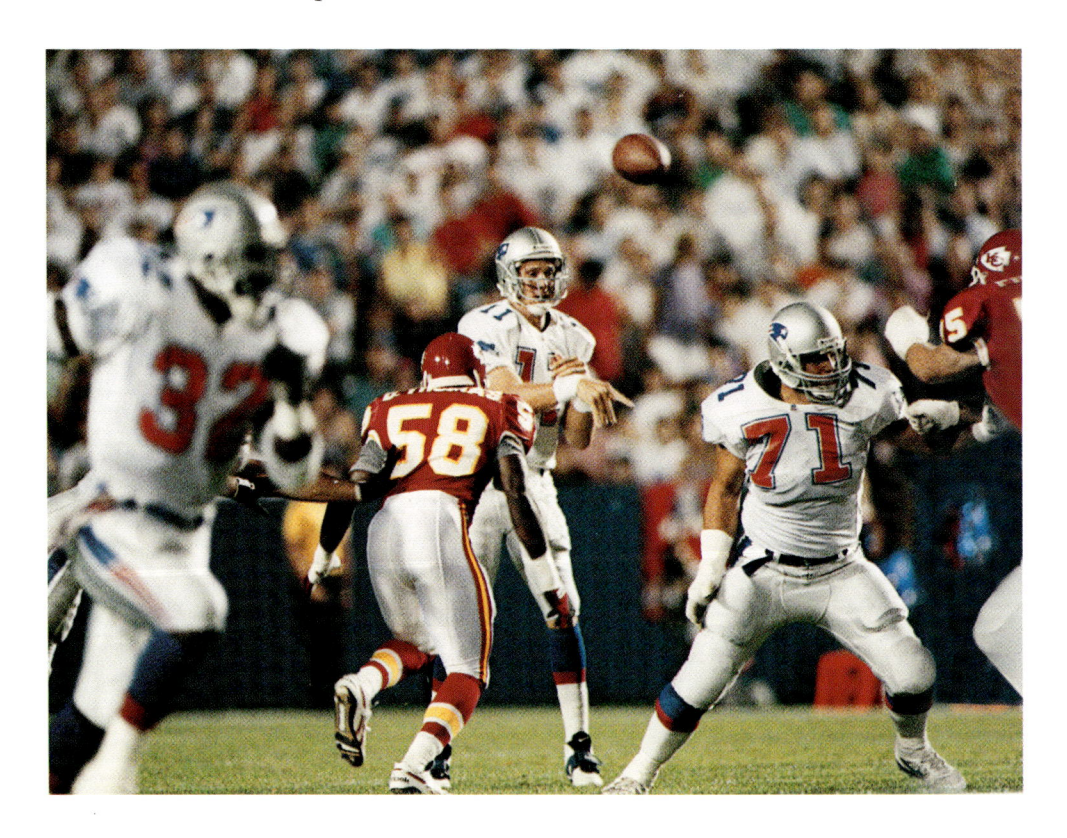

Quarterback Drew Bledsoe gets off a pass over Kansas City Chiefs linebacker Derrick Thomas (58).

game, New England trailed 20-10. But Bledsoe rallied the Patriots to snap their four-game losing streak.

Bledsoe passed for 426 yards and three touchdowns and was not intercepted or sacked. His 45 completions and 70 attempts were NFL records. He was 6-for-6 on the winning 67-yard drive.

Bledsoe teamed with running back Leroy Thompson on a 5-yard touchdown pass with 2:27 left in regulation to slice the Vikings lead to 20-10. Then he drove his team 56 yards for Matt Bahr's game-tying 23-yard field goal with 14 seconds left in regulation.

With 4:10 gone in overtime, Bledsoe lofted a 14-yard touchdown pass to fullback Kevin Turner—and New England shocked the Vikings 26-20.

"It was a valiant effort," Parcells said. "We were on the ropes big time."

The Patriots continued their comeback the following week. But this time, running back Marion Butts was the hero. He trampled his former San Diego teammates as the Patriots upset their second straight division leader, 23-17. Butts ran for a season-high 88 yards and one touchdown on 28 carries.

"I thought we played our best game of the year," Parcells said.

In Week 13, New England beat Indianapolis 12-10 as Bahr kicked four field goals and Bledsoe set a single-season Patriots passing yardage record.

Bledsoe was 26-for-36 for 271 yards and raised his season total to 3,526 yards, breaking the ream record of 3,465 by Babe Parilli in 1964.

Even better, New England won it third straight game, moving into a three-way tie with Buffalo and the Jets for second place in the AFC East—two games behind Miami with four games to go. Could they catch them?

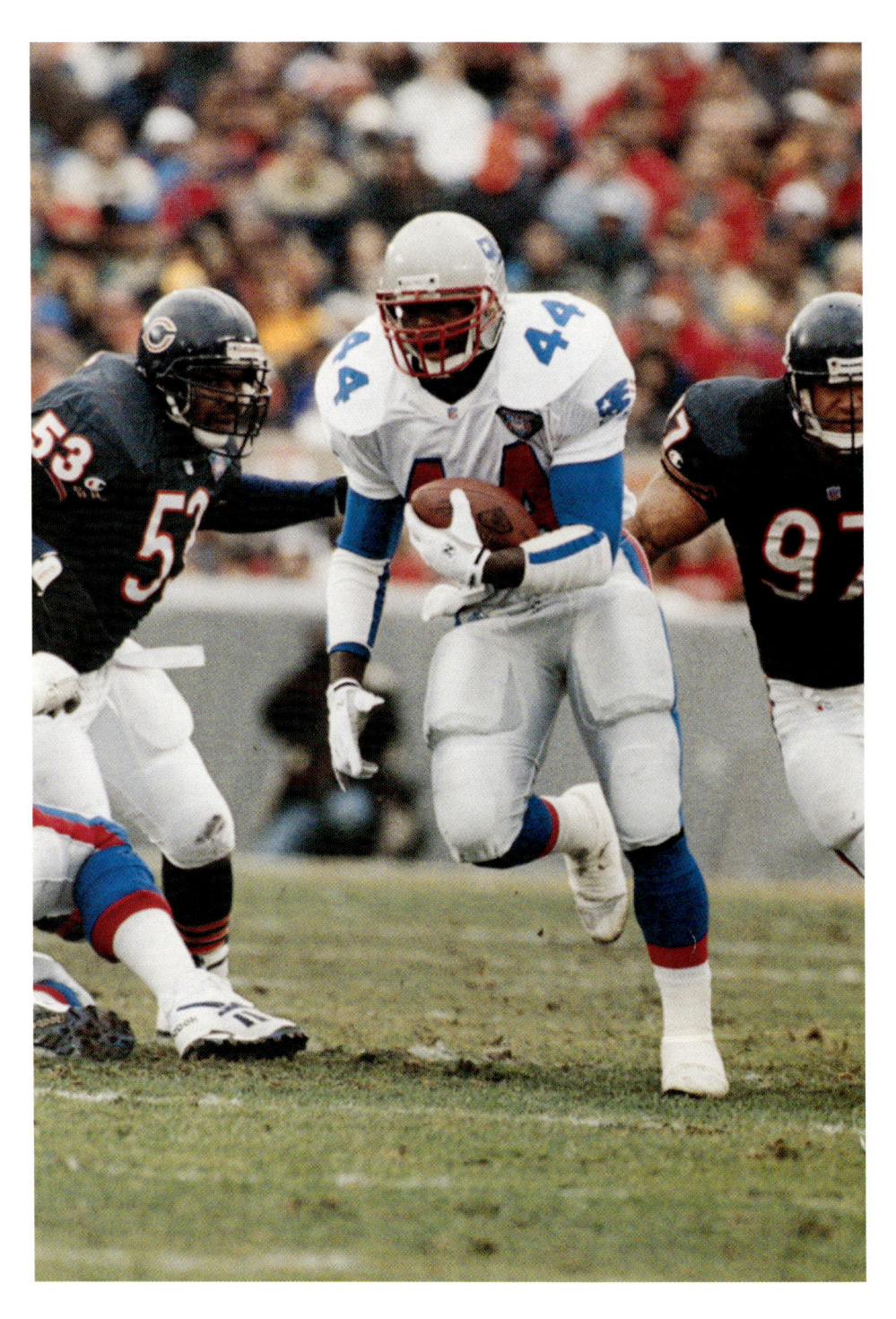

Running back Marion Butts (44) drives past Chicago Bears defenders for a 12-yard gain, December 1994.

The next week, in a crucial game against the Jets, the Patriots trailed 13-10 in the third quarter. Suddenly, New England defensive back Ricky Reynolds intercepted a pass by Boomer Esiason and dashed 11 yards for the score. It put New England ahead for good in a 24-13 victory. It was the Patriots fourth win in a row. At 7-6, New England was tied for second place with Buffalo—and only one game behind Miami.

In Week 15, the Patriots continued their amazing turnaround with a 28-13 victory over the Indianapolis Colts despite Bledsoe's four interceptions. He finished the day with 277 passing yards. With their fifth straight win, New England moved closer to their first playoff appearance in eight seasons. Their next opponent was the defending AFC champion Buffalo Bills.

At Buffalo, the drama was high. The Bills needed a win to stay in the playoff hunt. They had made the playoffs every year since 1987. A loss would eliminate them.

The Patriots were happy to send the Bills packing. Bledsoe passed for three touchdowns while cornerback Rickey Reynolds helped give his team a 31-17 lead with back-to-back fumble recoveries. Reynolds returned a fumble 25 yards for a touchdown, then recovered another to set up a touchdown. With their 41-17 rout of the Bills, New England moved into a first-place tie with Miami.

"Today was their finest hour so far," Parcells said of his team. With a win the following week in Chicago, the Patriots would make the playoffs. But the Bears were also fighting for a playoff spot. So a win would not be easy.

The Patriots clung to a 6-3 lead. Then Bledsoe put together a 51-yard touchdown drive to clinch the 13-3 win. The march ended with Bledsoe's 3-yard touchdown pass to running back Leroy Thompson with 2:32 left.

Bledsoe passed for 277 yards. He set an NFL single-season record for attempts (691). His 400 completions missed breaking the all-time mark by five yards.

Two years after taking over a team that went 2-14, Parcells had the Patriots in the playoffs with a seven-game winning streak. "This is as about as happy as I've been in a long time," he said after the game. But since they tied Miami with a 10-6 record, the Patriots had to settle for second place. The two regular-season losses to the Dolphins cost New England the divisional title.

The playoffs were not kind to the Patriots. They lost 20-13 to the Cleveland Browns. Bledsoe attempted 50 passes and completed only 21. He was also intercepted three times. He gave the Patriots a brief 7-3 lead in the second quarter with a 13-yard touchdown pass to Leroy Thompson. But the Cleveland defense shut him down the rest of the game.

§

Despite the playoff loss, New England is poised to make a run at the NFL championship. With talented young players like Bledsoe and Thompson, the offense will remain one of the league's best for a long time. Should the defense improve, the Patriots will undoubtedly capture their first Super Bowl victory.

GLOSSARY

ALL-PRO—A player who is voted to the Pro Bowl.
BACKFIELD—Players whose position is behind the line of scrimmage.
CORNERBACK—Either of two defensive halfbacks stationed a short distance behind the linebackers and relatively near the sidelines.
DEFENSIVE END—A defensive player who plays on the end of the line and often next to the defensive tackle.
DEFENSIVE TACKLE—A defensive player who plays on the line and between the guard and end.
ELIGIBLE—A player who is qualified to be voted into the Hall of Fame.
END ZONE—The area on either end of a football field where players score touchdowns.
EXTRA POINT—The additional one-point score added after a player makes a touchdown. Teams earn extra points if the placekicker kicks the ball through the uprights of the goalpost, or if an offensive player crosses the goal line with the football before being tackled.
FIELD GOAL—A three-point score awarded when a placekicker kicks the ball through the uprights of the goalpost.
FULLBACK—An offensive player who often lines up farthest behind the front line.
FUMBLE—When a player loses control of the football.
GUARD—An offensive lineman who plays between the tackles and center.
GROUND GAME—The running game.
HALFBACK—An offensive player whose position is behind the line of scrimmage.
HALFTIME—The time period between the second and third quarters of a football game.
INTERCEPTION—When a defensive player catches a pass from an offensive player.
KICK RETURNER—An offensive player who returns kickoffs.
LINEBACKER—A defensive player whose position is behind the line of scrimmage.
LINEMAN—An offensive or defensive player who plays on the line of scrimmage.
PASS—To throw the ball.
PASS RECEIVER—An offensive player who runs pass routes and catches passes.
PLACEKICKER—An offensive player who kicks extra points and field goals. The placekicker also kicks the ball from a tee to the opponent after his team has scored.

PLAYOFFS—The postseason games played amongst the division winners and wild card teams which determines the Super Bowl champion.
PRO BOWL—The postseason All-Star game which showcases the NFL's best players.
PUNT—To kick the ball to the opponent.
QUARTER—One of four 15-minute time periods that makes up a football game.
QUARTERBACK—The backfield player who usually calls the signals for the plays.
REGULAR SEASON—The games played after the preseason and before the playoffs.
ROOKIE—A first-year player.
RUNNING BACK—A backfield player who usually runs with the ball.
RUSH—To run with the football.
SACK—To tackle the quarterback behind the line of scrimmage.
SAFETY—A defensive back who plays behind the linemen and linebackers. Also, two points awarded for tackling an offensive player in his own end zone when he's carrying the ball.
SPECIAL TEAMS—Squads of football players that perform special tasks (for example, kickoff team and punt-return team).
SPONSOR—A person or company that finances a football team.
SUPER BOWL—The NFL Championship game played between the AFC champion and the NFC champion.
T FORMATION—An offensive formation in which the fullback lines up behind the center and quarterback with one halfback stationed on each side of the fullback.
TACKLE—An offensive or defensive lineman who plays between the ends and the guards.
TAILBACK—The offensive back farthest from the line of scrimmage.
TIGHT END—An offensive lineman who is stationed next to the tackles, and who usually blocks or catches passes.
TOUCHDOWN—When one team crosses the goal line of the other team's end zone. A touchdown is worth six points.
TURNOVER—To turn the ball over to an opponent either by a fumble, an interception, or on downs.
UNDERDOG—The team that is picked to lose the game.
WIDE RECEIVER—An offensive player who is stationed relatively close to the sidelines and who usually catches passes.
WILD CARD—A team that makes the playoffs without winning its division.
ZONE PASS DEFENSE—A pass defense method where defensive backs defend a certain area of the playing field rather than individual pass receivers.

INDEX

A

AFC championship 4, 13
AFC Eastern Division 13

B

Bahr, Matt 22, 25
Baltimore Colts 15
Bell, Upton 9
Berry, Raymond 13, 15
Bledsoe, Drew 4, 21, 22, 23, 24, 25, 27, 28
Boston Patriots 6
Buffalo Bills 6, 22, 27
Buoniconti, Nick 6
Butts, Marion 25

C

Cappelletti, Gino 6
Cincinnati Bengals 22
Clayborn, Raymond 10
Coates, Ben 22
Collins, Tony 15
Cook, Marv 20
Crittenden, Ray 23
Cunningham, Sam 9

D

Detroit Lions 22
Dykes, Hart Lee 17

E

Eason, Tony 13, 15
Elway, John 16
Erhardt, Ron 13
Esiason, Boomer 27

F

Fairbanks, Chuck 9, 13
Fox, Tim 13
Foxboro, Massachusetts 8
Francis, Russ 10, 13
Fryar, Irving 4, 15, 17, 20

G

Gray, Leon 12
Grogan, Steve 4, 10, 13, 15, 16, 20

H

Hannah, John 9, 12, 16
Harvard University 8
Haynes, Michael 4, 10, 12
Holovak, Mike 6
Houston Oilers 13

J

James, Craig 15

K

Kelly, Jim 22

L

Lippett, Ronnie 17
Los Angeles Raiders 15

M

MacPherson, Dick 20, 21
Marino, Dan 22, 24
Mazur, John 9
Meyer, Ron 13
Miami Dolphins 15
Millen, Hugh 20
Morgan, Stanley 4, 12, 15, 16, 17

N

Nance, Jim 6-8
New Orleans Saints 12
New York Jets 15, 23

O

Oakland Raiders 9

P

Parcells, Bill 4, 21, 25, 27, 28
Parilli, Babe 6, 7, 25
passing records 4
Payton, Walter 15
Plunkett, Jim 9, 10

R

Reynolds, Ricky 27
Rookie of the Year 10, 20
Russell, Leonard 20, 21
Rust, Rod 17, 20

S

San Diego Chargers 6
San Francisco 49ers 10
Shoate, Rod 13
Sims, Kenneth 13
Stabler, Ken 10
Stephens, John 17
Stingley, Darryl 9, 13, 15
Sullivan, Billy 8, 13
Super Bowl 12, 15, 21, 28
Syracuse University 6, 20

T

Tatum, Jack 13
Taylor, Lawrence 17
Thompson, Leroy 25, 27, 28
Timpson, Michael 22
Tippett, Andre 4, 13, 17

U

University of Colorado 13
University of Iowa 13
University of Texas 12, 13

V

Veris, Garin 17

W

Williams, Brent 17

The New England Patriots
J 796.33 Ita   37448000606904

Italia, Bob
Rutland Free Public Library

Rutland Public Library
280 Main Street
Rutland, MA 01543
www.rutlandlibrary.org